Alfred Gurney

A Christmas faggot

Alfred Gurney

A Christmas faggot

ISBN/EAN: 9783743384224

Manufactured in Europe, USA, Canada, Australia, Japa

Cover: Foto ©Andreas Hilbeck / pixelio.de

Manufactured and distributed by brebook publishing software
(www.brebook.com)

Alfred Gurney

A Christmas faggot

A CHRISTMAS FAGGOT

A CHRISTMAS FAGGOT

BY

ALFRED GURNEY, M.A.

VICAR OF S. BARNABAS', PIMLICO

AUTHOR OF 'THE VISION OF THE EUCHARIST AND OTHER POEMS' ETC.

'The Darling of the world is come,
And fit it is we finde a roome
To welcome Him. The nobler part
Of all the house here is the heart,
Which we will give Him, and bequeat
This hollie and this ivie wreath
To do Him honour who's our King,
The Lord of all this revelling'

HERRICK, *A Christmas Carol*

LONDON

KEGAN PAUL, TRENCH, & CO., 1 PATERNOSTER SQUARE

1884

MY GODCHILDREN

ETHEL,	ALBINIA,
CYRIL,	BASIL,
BERTRAM,	WILFRID,
LOUISE,	HELEN,

ARTHUR.

When the Angel of the waters
　With a gold and silver wing
Gently stirred the wave baptismal,
　Heard ye not their carolling
Who of old to Eastern shepherds
　Heralded their King?

To the shepherds of His people
　Still those angel-voices tell
How God's river feeds the fountain
　Opened by Emmanuel,
Yielding the baptismal waters
　Of salvation's well.

Children, you have passed those waters,
　Love-begotten from the dead ;
Will you make a gallant promise
　When my verses you have read—
'We will trace life's lovely river
　To the Fountain-head'?

Loch Leven : 1884.

PREFACE.

Most of the following poems have appeared in the 'S. Barnabas' Parish Magazine.' For my godchildren and my people I have made them up into a little bundle of sticks—a Christmas faggot to feed the fires in the winter palace of our King.

It is the Incarnation that justifies all joy, and song is the expression of joy. The Gospel Songs all celebrate the Great Nativity. Birth and marriage are the occasions most sacred to mirth and music among men ; and Christmas is at once the Birthday and the Marriage Festival of Humanity.

Glad and thankful shall I be if any song of mine should help to fan the flame of rejoicing love in any Christian heart at this holy and happy season.

CONTENTS.

—◦•◦—

	PAGE
YULE TIDE	1
THE MADONNA DI SAN SISTO	6
BETHLEHEM GATE	11
SAINT JOSEPH	16
A CRADLE SONG	18
A CRADLED CHILD	23
AN EMPTY CRADLE	26
NEW YEAR'S EVE	28
THE VICTIM	30
THE DAYSMAN	33
THE PHYSICIAN	36

CONTENTS

	PAGE
THE POET	40
THREE SISTERS	43
A CHRISTMAS PUZZLE	46
FOUR EPIPHANIES	48
THE CHILDREN'S EUCHARIST	56
THE GOSPEL SONGS :	
I. Benedictus	59
II. Magnificat	63
III. Nunc Dimittis	66
NOTES	69

YULE TIDE.

'They bring me sorrow touched with joy,
    The merry merry bells of Yule.'

                    TENNYSON, *In Memoriam.*

THE Royal Birthday dawns again,

    A stricken world to bless ;

And sufferers forget their pain,

    And mourners their distress.

Love sings to-day ; her eyes so fair

    With happy tears are wet ;

She is too humble to despair,

    Too faithful to forget.

B

Her voice is very soft and sweet,
    Her heart is brave and strong ;
Her vassal, I would fain repeat
    Some fragments of her song.

A Birthday-song my heart would sing
    Its rapture to express ;
My Father's son must be a king,
    And share His consciousness.

Of God's Self-knowledge comes the Word
    That utters all His Thought ;
That Word made Flesh by all is heard
    Who seek as they are sought.

His seeking and His finding make

    Our search an easy thing ;

He sows good seed, and bids us take

    The joys of harvesting.

Yet must His children do their part,

    And what He gives accept :

No heart can understand His Heart

    That has not bled and wept.

All seasons, bring they bale or bliss,

    His priceless treasures hold ;

The Winter's silver all is His,

    And His the Summer's gold.

Life's harvest is not reaped until
    The Christ within has grown
To perfect manhood, and self-will
    By love is overthrown.

Such manhood gained concludes the strife
    That makes the babe a boy;
'Tis thus the seed becomes a life
    The life becomes a joy.

The eyes that weep are eyes that see,
    And swift are pilgrim-feet;
Ah! hope at length may come to be
    Than memory more sweet.

So keeping festival to-day,

   With children's laughter near,

It is not hard to sing and pray,

   'T is hard to doubt or fear.

Father, my heart to Thee I bring,

   To Thee my song address ;

From Winter pain and toil of Spring

   Grows Summer happiness.

THE MADONNA DI SAN SISTO.[1]

'The Lord Himself shall give you a sign; behold, a Virgin shall conceive and bear a Son.'

BEHOLD, by Raphael shown, Love's sacrament!

Earth's curtains part, God's veil is lifted up;

There comes a Child, forth from His Bosom sent

To rule the feast of life, His Bread and Cup,

His purpose making plain with man to sup.

Out-streams the light, accomplished is the Sign,

A Virgin-Mother clasps a Babe Divine.

[1] *See* Note A, page 60.

Her lovely feet descend the cloudy stair,

   Great succour bringing to a world forlorn,

On either side a man and woman share

   A common rapture, welcoming the dawn

   Of God's new day, the everlasting morn—

Of such a day as shall from East to West

Dispel the darkness, doing Love's behest.

He turns a face all radiant to the Sun,

   Enamoured of the sight he looks upon ;

She to the end of what is now begun

   Downgazes, stooping, shadowed by the throne

   Made by a Maiden's arms, maternal grown ;

Than ivory most fair, than purest gold,

More pure, more fair, and stronger to uphold.

On cherubs twain, whom watching has made wise,

A spell has fallen—a prophetic dream ;

Their upward-gazing and far-seeing eyes,

Like stars reflected in a tranquil stream,

To look beyond the Child and Mother seem ;

A twisted thorn-branch and a cross to them

Are manifest—His throne and diadem.

High heaven open stands, and there a crowd

Of worshippers with love-lit eyes appear,

Like stars down-gazing through a fleecy cloud,

Dimly discerned as morning draweth near

Spreading a radiant pall upon night's bier.

The blessed thing the Sign doth signify

They partly know, and are made glad thereby.

But more the Mother knows, and more she

  sees

  Than soaring angel or than climbing saint ;

Her heart familiar grown with mysteries

  Of God's own working under love's con-

  straint,

  The remedy she knows for man's complaint.

The clouds are all beneath her, and above

The light of life, the radiancy of love.

And He, Whom Lord of love and life we hail,

   Is on her bosom borne, a blossom fair ;

The pentecostal breath that lifts her veil

   Has fanned His royal brow, and stirred His hair,

   And kissed His lips just parted for a prayer.

That spirit-wind shall blow, that Face shall shine,

Till all His brothers know their Father's Sign.

   Dresden : 1883.

BETHLEHEM GATE.

A Picture by Dante Gabriel Rossetti.[1]

OF old through gates that closed on them
    Two exiles went with eyes downcast ;
    The Present now retrieves the Past,
God's Eden is in Bethlehem.

An Eden that no walls enclose
    By Mary's arms encompassèd,
    A living shrine, a 'house of bread,'
A very haven of repose.

[1] *See* Note D, page 71.

Behold the Prince of Peace! around
　　His cradle angry tempests rage ;
　　He needs must go on pilgrimage,
An exile, homeless and discrowned.

And yet, His Rank to designate,
　　The unquenched Star of Bethlehem
　　Shines forth, a radiant diadem ;
While Angels on His footsteps wait.

E'en now the Father's Face they see,
　　A triumph-song e'en now they sing,
　　And, wondering and worshipping,
Attend His Pilgrim-Family.

Two guard the frowning gateway: one

   Is of a solemn countenance ;

   To him a rapid backward glance

Reveals a massacre begun.

The other, forward gazing, sees

   The glory of the age to come,

   The fruitfulness of martyrdom,

Of deaths that are nativities.

O weeping mothers, dry your tears !

   The Mother whom this canvass shows

   Nor fears, nor weeps, although she knows

An anguish deeper than your fears.

She knows a comfort deeper still

For all who fare on pilgrimage ;

By suffering from age to age

God seals the vassals of His Will.

Her Burden is upholding her ;

And, guided by the Holy Dove,

She sees the victory of Love

Beyond the Cross and Sepulchre.

To shield her, Joseph stands : his care

The shadow of God's Providence.

How fragrant is the frankincense

Of their uninterrupted prayer!

Through ever-open gates they press,

   A new and living way they tread,

   So gain they the true ' House of Bread,'

A garden for a wilderness.

A flight it seems to us ; to them

   It is a going forth to win

   The world from Satan and from sin,

And build the New Jerusalem.

Lord Christ ! for every seeking soul

   Thou art Thyself the Door, the Way,

   All, all shall find one coming day

Thy Heart their everlasting goal !

Loch Leven : 1884.

S. JOSEPH.

A CLOISTERED garden was the place
  Where Mary grew, God's perfect flower;
One, only one, discerned her grace,
  And visited her bower.

God's choice was his; by love made strong
  To guard the Mother of the King;
No heart, save hers, had e'er a song
  So sweet as his to sing.

Yet lives there on the sacred page

No record of a word from him :

God's Ark he guards, a silent sage,

Pure as the Cherubim.

But sweeter than the sweetest word

Recorded of the wise and good,

His silence is a music heard

On high, and understood.

Blessed are all who take their part

Amid the carol-singing throng ;

Thrice blest the meditative heart

Whose silence is a song.

BALLACHULISH : 1884.

A CRADLE SONG.

SING, ye winds, and sing, ye waters,
  May the music of your song
Silence all the dark forebodings
  That have plagued the world too long;
He who made your voices tuneful
  Comes to right the wrong.

Warble on, ye feathered songsters,
  Lift your praises loud and high,

Merry lark, and thrush, and blackbird,

In the grove and in the sky

Make your music, shame our dumbness,

Till we make reply.

Children's laughter is a music

Flowing from a hidden spring,

Which, though men misdoubt its virtue,

Well is worth discovering ;

Slowly dies the heart that knows not

How to laugh and sing.

Hark, a cradle-song ! the Singer

Is the Heart of God Most High ;

All sweet voices are the echoes

    That in varied tones reply

To that Voice which through the ages

    Sings earth's lullaby.

Oftentimes a sleepless infant

    For a season frets and cries :

All at once an unseen finger

    Curtains up the little eyes.

So the cradled child He nurses

    God will tranquillise.

His the all-enfolding Presence :

    Oh, what tutelage it brings

To the little lives that ripen

    'Neath the shelter of its wings ;

God's delays are no denials,

    As He waits He sings !

They alone are seers and singers

    Who invalidate despair

By the lofty hopes they cherish,

    By the gallant deeds they dare,

By the ceaseless aspirations

    Of a life of prayer.

Brothers, sisters, lift your voices,

    May the rapture of your song

A CRADLE SONG

Put to flight the sad misgivings
   That have vexed the world too long ;
God would have us share the triumph
   That shall right the wrong.

Loch Laggan : 1884.

A CRADLED CHILD.

(To E. A. G.)

BEHOLD! the world's inheritance,
 The treasure-trove of happy homes;
 Whereby the poorest hut becomes
A fairy-palace of romance.

A cradle is the mother's shrine:
 Two lamps o'erhang it—her sweet eyes,
 Whose love-light falls, Madonna-wise,
On sleeping infancy divine.

The presence of a ' holy thing,'

  Madonna-wise, her heart discerns,

  And like a fragrant censer burns,

O'ershadowed by an angel's wing.

Her brooding motherhood is strong ;

  A trembling joy her bosom stirs,

  Her thoughts are white-robed worshippers,

' Magnificat ' is all her song.

'Mid angels whispering ' all-hails '

  The waking moment she awaits,

  The opening of two pearly gates,

The lifting of two silken veils.

Ah! then, what words can tell the bliss,

The rapture of the fond embrace,

When mother's lips on baby's face,

Feast and are feasted with a kiss?

And who can tell of hands and feet

The dimpled wonders, hidden charms,

The dainty curves of legs and arms,

So sweet and soft, so soft and sweet?

This is the world's possession still,

The treasure-trove of wedded hearts,

Whereby a Father's love imparts

His joy, their gladness to fulfil.

TYNTESFIELD: 1884.

AN EMPTY CRADLE.

ALL empty stands a little cradle-bed,

 A mother's falling tears the only sound ;

 But not of earth her thoughts, nor underground ;

Up-gazing she discerns the Fountain-head

Of life ; the living Voice she hears that said

 ' Fear not ' to weeping women who had found

 An empty tomb, and angels watching round,

Who asked ' Why seek the living with the dead ? '

So weeps our Mother Church—her tears outshine

  Sun-smitten dewdrops on a summer's morn ;

God's rainbow girdles her, Hope's lovely sign,

  Whereby she knows that smiles of tears are

    born ;

Fulfilled of life herself, she would assure

Her children all of death's discomfiture.

CARLISLE : 1884.

NEW YEAR'S EVE.

GOD grant through coming years and days
  Our beating hearts may be
The harps that celebrate His praise
  Who loves eternally!

No ache can be without relief
  When Love Himself draws near;
No cup can empty stand, no grief
  Embitter God's New Year.

NEW YEAR'S EVE

Time's footsteps quickly die away,
   Soon emptied is his glass ;
We wait for an oncoming Day
   Which nevermore shall pass.

Old hopes revive, new hopes are born,
   The coming months to cheer ;
And phantom-fears and griefs outworn
   Die with the dying year.

Oh, all the years and all the days
   Our waiting hearts shall be
Harps tremulous with His dear praise
   Whose is Eternity !

S. BARNABAS' : *December* 31, 1883.

THE VICTIM.

For the Feast of the Circumcision : New Year's Day.

THE sun methinks rose rosy-red
   On that great New Year's Day,
When Blood was in the cradle shed
   Where Mary's Darling lay.

The lark, uprising with the sun,
   Was silent on the wing ;
The nightingale, when day was done,
   Forgot her song to sing.

A holy silence reigned around,

   And hushed was every voice,

When in the crib the Cross was found,

   The Infant-Victim's choice.

As moonbeam on a mountain-mere

   The Mother's face was white;

Her eyes were stars, and every tear

   Gave lustre to their light.

Methinks a blushing moon looked down

   Upon that manger-bed,

And wove a mystic glory-crown

   Around the Sleeper's head.

The silence issues in a song,

   It rises and it swells ;

E'en than the lark's more blithe and strong,

   Sweeter than Philomel's,

His Church's anthem loud and long

   The Victim's triumph tells.

THE DAYSMAN.

IN boyhood's sorrow-shadowed days,

    Which memory recalls to-day,

In many moods and many ways,

    My yearning heart would pray.

'Twas holy ground where'er I set

    My feet, God's shrine was everywhere ;

But this I scarcely knew as yet—

    Christ is His Father's Prayer.[1]

[1] *See* Note C, page 72.

God ever seeks His children's bliss,
    Appeals to them ; and, rightly heard.
The music of creation is
    The echo of His Word.

But when the child has learnt his part,
    The echo is an answer strong ;
A prayer up-springing from the heart
    That blossoms in a song.

Christ is the Living Word of God,
    His Poem and His Prophecy ;
The homeward way His Feet have trod
    Mankind must travel by.

And every man, God's child and priest,

    Is pledged to ministry divine,

Who sees the Ruler of life's feast

    Turn water into wine ;

Who hears the Father's voice above,

    The Spirit's whispering within ;

Who knows the Messenger of love

    The Conqueror of sin.

Responsive to God's call, our Prayer

    Art Thou, dear Lord, whene'er we pray ;

So always now, and everywhere,

    My heart keeps holiday.

On the Danube :
   Feast of the Holy Name, 1883.

THE PHYSICIAN.

Is life sad for lost love's sake,

    Falls a blight upon thy bliss,

Smiles no more their sunshine make,

    Lips estranged withhold their kiss?

For thy consolation take

    Some such song as this :—

Shine on us, O Morning Star!

    Help our weeping eyes to see;

Never may we deem things are

    What to us they seem to be :

Rise, Thou Dayspring, and afar.

    Bid the shadows flee !

Jesu, Thou art swift to bless,

    Strong to comfort, skilled to heal ;

Failure is with Thee success,

    Woe the forerunner of weal ;

Every stroke is a caress,

    Every crust a meal.

Master, Thou canst raise the dead

    From the grave, the bed, the bier,[1]

---

[1] S. John xi. 43 ; S. Matt. ix. 25 ; S. Luke vii. 14.

Souls astray, forlorn, misled,

   Buffeted by doubt and fear,

Cannot but be comforted

   When Thou drawest near.

Sweeter than the Sunday-bells

   Banishing all week-day cares,

Thine the gracious voice that tells

   What a Father's love prepares,

Leading to salvation's wells

   Up God's altar-stairs.

Lord, Thou art the Master-singer,

   And Thy song is a recall ;

Many on life's pathway linger,

Many by life's wayside fall,

But Thy Heart, the comfort-bringer,

Is a Home for all!

TYROL : 1882.

THE POET.

THE poet is the child of God,
  Who with anointed eye
Discerns a sacrament of love
  In earth and sea and sky,
And finds himself at love's behest
  Constrained to prophesy.

Love is of loveliness the root,
  Love is of life the spring,

Love is the sole interpreter
  Of every lovely thing :
This is the burden of his song,
  Well may the poet sing !

A joy-inspirèd song he sings
  Because far off he hears
A whisper silencing the storm,
  A laughter through the tears,
The music of eternity
  Beyond the dying years.

His song is rapture, for he sees
  God's loveliness, and we,

When with his insight we are blest,

    Shall share his ecstasy ;

Oh, come the day when all shall sing

    As blithe a song as he!

Lord Christ, Thou art the King of Love,

    Thou art the Poet true ;

The men who would Thy vision share

    Must learn Thy works to do,

All, all shall have the singing heart

    Whose feet Thy steps pursue !

Fitz Ortler : 1882.

THREE SISTERS.[1]

THREE fountains clear as crystal spring
  In one secluded garden-plot ;
  In shade and shelter of one cot
Three sister-doves are harbouring.

Adown one pathway hand in hand
  Three Sister-Graces wend their way ;
  I shall not soon forget the day
I met with them in fairy land.

[1] *See* Note D, page 74.

They *dazzled*, I know not how or whence

    A halo circling round the head

    Of each, whereby transfigurèd

They clomb the hill of frankincense.

I know not whence or how, they *bloomed*:

    Each sweeter than the sweetest rose

    That in the haunted garden grows

Where burns the bush still unconsumed.

And one is like a rising sun

    When dewy Morn unveils her eyes;

    And one is as Minerva wise;

And very lily-like is one.

And all are dear.   I seem to see

The weaving of a threefold cord—

To hear a softly whispered word,

' Love makes a unity of three.'

A CHRISTMAS PUZZLE.

(For Grown-up Children.)

Children know the things I know not,
  Though they know not that they know :
I should know not, should love grow not,
  That I know not it is so.
Flowers feebly rooted blow not,
Shallow waters overflow not,
  Love is doomed unless it grow.

Fools who think to reap and sow not

    Growing love will overthrow ;

Churls who say 'We go' and go not

    Love's rebuke must undergo ;

All who love's insignia show not,

Who on love themselves bestow not,

    Love, full grown, shall lay them low.

FOUR EPIPHANIES.

I.

THE Pilgrim-Kings their King have found,
   The Wise Men kneel at Wisdom's shrine,
Their royal gifts His Crib surround,
   He gives them bread and wine.

One Star has pointed to the Sun,
   That men may see and understand
The witness borne by all to One,
   Who holds in His Right Hand,

¹ *See* Note E, page 77.

Like lamps that round an altar burn,

   All lights that shine, all worlds that be

Crowned are the men whose hearts discern

   Their King's Epiphany.

II.

THE Child obedient sets His face
    To seek His Father's House of Prayer,
With other children takes His place,
    And is a learner there.

Two worlds there are ; the child to each
    Belongs, God's prophet, born to bless ;
But not by action, nor by speech,
    Simply by winsomeness.

For, like the Child of Bethlehem,

  Babes bring their blessing from afar,

Enriching all who wait on them

  By being what they are.

III.

A VOICE from heaven spake aloud,
    Heard clearly by the Bridegroom's friend
When, shadowed by the glory-cloud,
    He saw the Dove descend.

One Voice has heralded the Word,
    That listening men may truly know
What mean all voices they have heard
    Above, around, below—

FOUR EPIPHANIES

Soft whisperings and laughters loud,

   The song of birds, the insects' hum,

Storm-music of the thunder-cloud --

   And be no longer dumb.

IV.

That jubilance of bridal mirth,

    First felt at Cana, has not ceased ;

Christ's Presence still regales the earth,

    Still glorifies the feast.

The Ruler of the feast of life

    Still with a sacramental sign

Confirms the love of man and wife,

    And makes the water wine.

And His the glory still revealed

When lovers plight and keep their vows :

Himself the Bridegroom Who has sealed

The Church to be His Spouse.

THE CHILDREN'S EUCHARIST.

THE children's star-crowned Bethlehem,
  The children's ' house of bread,'
Where Jesus' arms encircle them,
  With milk and honey fed :—
Such is the Church, whose altar-gates
  Stand ever open, when
The board is furnished where He waits
  To feast the hearts of men.

A Babe He came one heart to bless
  (It is His cradle still),
And evermore her blessedness
  Is theirs who do His will ;
A Child He trod the Temple-floor,
  By Mary Mother led ;
By children's voices evermore
  His praise is perfected.

' Forbid them not,' He said of old :
  The words so stern and sweet
Still make believing mothers bold
  To gather at His Feet,

And bring their babes ; their hearts discern

(And oh, that others would !)

How mother-like His Heart must yearn

Who made their motherhood.

A happy Home where children pray,

With milk and honey fed,

Whose altar-hearth burns bright alway,

Whose board is richly spread :—

Such is the Church ; and sweet the song

Her little children sing,

Of all who round His Altar throng

The dearest to our King.

BALLACHULISH : 1884.

THE GOSPEL SONGS.[1]

I.

BENEDICTUS.

CAN priestly lips, long silenced, raise

A strain so lofty and so strong,

Making our matin hymn of praise

As jubilant as evensong ?

Yes : not the lips alone, the eyes

Of Zacharias were unsealed,

To see and sing the mysteries

To love and penitence revealed.

[1] See Note F, page 78.

With keen prevision of the seer
 He sings of a redemption wrought,
Whereby, released from slavish fear,
 Men are to filial freedom brought.

Three things immutable and sure,
 His promise, covenant, and oath,
Reveal God's purpose, and secure
 Whate'er man needs for life and growth.

The promise to the fathers made
 Was seen and known—th' Incarnate Word ;
The Cross His covenant displayed,
 His oath at Pentecost was heard.

Well may this father's heart rejoice,

    And with prophetic rapture sing ;

His song a prelude to that ' Voice ' [1]

    Predestined to proclaim the King.

His joy a foretaste of that mirth

    Which shall the hearts of all possess,

When o'er a recreated earth

    Christ's sceptre reigns in righteousness.

Of light he sings for darkened eyes,

    For wandering feet the way of peace,

Tells how the Dayspring shall arise,

    And shadows flee and sorrows cease.

[1] S. John i. 23.

And still the Church's children raise

That strain so lofty and so strong,

Which makes their matin hymn of praise

As jubilant as evensong.

Loch Laggan : 1884.

II.

MAGNIFICAT.

EARTH'S noise God's music supersedes,
   Sin's discord it excludes,
It tells us of a Lamb that bleeds,
   And of a Dove that broods.

It tells us of a Child Who brings
   The help that sets us free ;
The song His Maiden-Mother sings
   Of saved Humanity.

The Mother's and the Sister's part
  She plays ; she leads the choir
Of those whose purity of heart
  Is passionate desire.

Above the blood-encrimsoned sea,
  Dispelling doubt and fear
With her celestial minstrelsy,
  Our Miriam doth cheer

The men whose homeward-going hearts
  Are loyal to their King ;
When all from her have learnt their parts,
  Then shall creation sing !

The sweetest of the Gospel songs,

    To all the Saints so dear,

To every eventide belongs

    Throughout the changeful year.

It sanctifies the vesper hour

    When summer smiles serene,

It is a joy-constraining power

    When winter blasts are keen.

' My soul doth magnify the Lord '

    Ecstatic is the voice

That sings of Paradise restored

    ' My spirit doth rejoice ! '

PINZOLO : 1882.

III.

NUNC DIMITTIS.

To cradle Mary's Child his heart
    An old man opens wide :
Behold him in God's peace depart,
    And in God's peace abide.

He sings the very Song of Peace,
    Responsive to the Word ;
His lullaby shall never cease
    To make its music heard

For all the children of the Bride,

    The subjects of the King,

With each returning eventide

    Have learnt his song to sing.

He sings of ' peace,' ' salvation,' ' light : '

    His lovely words we take

For consolation night by night,

    Until God's morning break.

Then, when our dazzled eyes grow dim,

    Breathed with our parting breath

The old man's sweet, heart-soothing hymn

    Glad welcome gives to death.

We too what Simeon saw may see —

The Mother undefiled,

Our hearts enfold as blissfully

The Everlasting Child!

TYROL: 1882.

NOTES.

———•✂•———

The Madonna di San Sisto.

Raffaelle's world-famous picture of the Mother and her Divine Child in the Gallery at Dresden is in a measure known to almost all from prints and photographs. As to the *colour* of the picture, the significant beauty of which none who have not seen the original can conceive, it should be remembered that the parted curtains are green (the earth-colour), and the Virgin Mother comes forth, as it were, from the white bosom of a stooping heaven, whose far distances, dimly seen, fade into a blue firmament peopled with angelic faces.

Many have felt this picture—at once so serene and so impassioned—to be a *revelation*. As we yield ourselves to its fascination and search further and further into its depths, we feel that Faber's words justify themselves : ' Christian Art, rightly considered, is at once a theology and a worship ; a theology which has its own method of teaching, its own ways of representation, its own devout discoveries, its own varying opinions, all of which are beautiful so long as they are in subordination to the mind of the Church. . . . Art is a revelation from heaven, and a mighty power for God. It is a merciful disclosure to men of His more hidden beauty. It brings out things in God which lie too deep for words.' (*Bethlehem*, p. 240.)

It was a satisfaction to find my reading of this incomparable picture powerfully endorsed by one who, more perhaps than any living writer, has made good his claim to be regarded with the reverence that belongs to a scribe instructed in the things of the spiritual kingdom, bringing forth from his treasure things new and old. I quote the following passage from Canon Westcott's weighty contribution to the discussion of a subject second to none in interest and importance -- 'The Relation of Christianity to Art :' 'In the *Madonna di San Sisto* Raffaelle has rendered the idea of Divine motherhood and Divine Sonship in intelligible forms. No one can rest in the individual figures. The tremulous fulness of emotion in the face of the Mother, the intense, far-reaching gaze of the Child, constrain the beholder to look beyond. For him too the curtain is drawn aside ; he feels that there is a fellowship of earth with heaven and of heaven with earth, and understands the meaning of the attendant Saints who express the different aspects of this double communion.' (*Epistles of S. John*, p. 358.)

I will only add some beautiful words of Mrs. Jameson, which also I had not seen when my verses were written: 'I have seen my own ideal once, and only once, attained : there, where Raffaelle—inspired if ever painter was inspired—projected on the space before him that wonderful creation which we style the *Madonna di San Sisto*; for there she stands—the transfigured woman—at once completely human and completely divine, an abstraction of power, purity, and love, poised on the empurpled air, and requiring no other support ; looking out with her melancholy, loving mouth, her slightly dilated, sibylline eyes, quite through the universe, to the end and consummation of all things : sad, as if she beheld afar off the visionary sword that was to reach her heart through Him, now resting as enthroned on that heart : yet already exalted through the homage of the redeemed generations who were to salute her as Blessed.' (*Legends of the Madonna* : Introduction, p. 44.)

NOTE B.

Bethlehem Gate.

I extract the following from some unpublished notes on the pictures by Rossetti exhibited at Burlington House two years ages : ' " Bethlehem Gate " is the name of a lovely little pictured parable. On the left we see the massacre of innocents, representing the world, in whose cruel habitations the same outrage is ever being enacted, since all sin is in truth the sin of blood-guiltiness, bringing life into jeopardy. On the right the Heavenly Dove is seen leading forth God's elect children, the Holy Family, the infant Church, to the land of righteousness. The Maiden-Mother, with the Divine Innocent enthroned on her bosom, attended and protected by a backward-looking and a forward-looking angel, and escorted by S. Joseph, passes the gate of the City of David. Egypt beneath her feet becomes the holy land.' Thus with all fitting ceremonial is the Church's pilgrimage through the world, through the ages, inaugurated.'

Note C.

The Daysman.

'The Word became Flesh and tabernacled among us' that is the supreme and august Verity which dominates all the thoughts of the children of the Kingdom. Their eyes are fixed on the Life that the Scripture-record contains rather than on the record itself.

See Isaiah xix. 19-25.

To them the oracles of God are indeed *living*, because they
discern therein not certain words about Christ, but Christ the
Word Himself; reading them by the light of the great Tradition
which lives and grows with the life and growth of the Spirit-
bearing Church – the consciousness of the real Presence of Christ
in her and in her Scriptures alike. It is in truth no unwritten
Tradition, for it is inscribed in spiritual characters upon the
fleshy tables of the heart by the Holy Ghost Himself, the Finger
of God. To His pupils all things are Divine *words* variously
embodied, and the Word made Flesh is the one all-comprehending
Mystery, the eternal, all-revealing, and all-sufficing Sacrament.
That Word is a Divine Person, Whose Manhood is a living, abiding, ever-energising Mediatorial Agency. That Word, eternally
uttered by the Mouth of God, was in the Incarnation uttered (so
to speak) in another language, and made audible and intelligible to man. By this language, common to God and man, the
thought of God became man's thought, and the thought of
man God's thought. In Him, the Mediating Word, they are *at
one*; He *is* the Atonement. And being the Word, He is the
Prayer both of God and man, whose expression is the enduring
evidence of that Atonement, the ceaseless occupation and satisfaction of those who in Him are atoned and united. 'A mediator
is not a mediator of one, but God is one,' is S. Paul's state-
ment of the mystery; and of this characteristic doctrine of
Christianity the Psalmist had already caught a glimpse when,

in the exercise of a prophetical gift, he speaks of Christ as *Prayer*.[1]

It is needless to add that the sanctuary of the Eucharist is the school in which this truth is most eloquently taught and effectually learnt.

Note D.

Three Sisters.

The following interpretation, which accompanied the poem on its first appearance, is retained for the sake of those who then welcomed it :—

Those who sing songs to children no less than they who tell them stories must be prepared for many questions, some of them difficult to answer. The two questions which recur most frequently are (1) 'Is it true ?' and (2) 'What does it mean ?'

Questioned as to my little poem, I reply to the first question without hesitation, — 'Yes, it is all true.' But the second question is more difficult to deal with. If, however, an answer is insisted on, something like this is what I must say :—

God's story has no end ; it is more wonderful than anything

Psalm cix. 4 : 'I am prayer' is the literal translation. KAY.

wonderland can show ; lovelier than the loveliest thing said or sung of fairyland. The Gospel and the Creed are a part of that story ; and with this our little poem is concerned. It speaks of God's garden—paradise regained a renewed earth, wherein a trinity in unity, observable in all things, testifies of Him, a shadow cast from above.

Shall we take the verses in order ?

Verse 1. Three fountains (which issue forth from beneath one altar-throne) feed one river (which, strange to say, seen from below, is four-fold), and by this river the whole earth, God's garden, is encircled and fertilised. That garden contains the tree of life, wherein three doves have one nest.

Verse 2. But the fuller revelation comes out of human nature itself, when taken into fellowship with God. The elect lady, representative of humanity, is from one point of view, looking at fundamental relations, daughter, spouse, mother ; from another, looking at essential characteristics, faith, hope, and love. The place of meeting, that is dawning consciousness, is the fairyland of phenomenal existence.

Verse 3. Out of this fairyland humanity is led forward and upward by the path of sacrifice, until the summit of the cross-crowned mountain of life is gained ; and all heads are aureoled by a light which, like that of the Transfiguration, dawns and deepens from within. This cannot be till we have ceased to be self-centred, and have become Christ-centred.

Verse 4. All growth is very secret and mysterious, part of the mystery of life. The development of humanity follows the order indicated in the narrative of creation; light must come before vegetation, sunshine before flowers. In the garden of the Incarnation all is recovered; the wilderness blossoms as a rose, and the poor bush of the desert becomes a garden-tree, a plant of renown, unconsumed because permanently enkindled with the fire of a divine life.

Verse 5. Every flower is a little sun, and shines forth, owing its beauty to an effort after conformity to the likeness of its cherisher, not without the succour of gracious dews. Its sunshine ministers to hope. And by faith the old-world homage rendered to wisdom (with which it is really one) is justified and transfigured. And love, being one with purity, looks at us out of the sweet white face of the lily.

Verse 6. All men, like these sister-graces, must join hands and hearts. Thus shall be woven a threefold cord, divinely strong and unbreakable; and the testimony, reiterated by the still small voice of a Divine Whisperer, shall be accepted by all, because realised in all: 'Love makes a unity of three;' and '*God is love.*'

'Is that what the poem means?' I think I hear my questioner ask. 'Yes, that is a little of what it means—only a little.'

NOTE E.

Four Epiphanies.

Nothing perhaps more clearly demonstrates the Divine instinct that resides in the Church than the construction of her Calendar and the arrangement of her year. Like the Creed, whose truths it teaches and enforces, it grew up gradually as the outcome and embodiment of her devotional life. The Epiphany, or Feast of Manifestation, was one of the first observed of her days of solemn commemoration ; and the day came to be prolonged into a season embracing six Sundays. She would have her children understand that in all that He did and said our Lord was manifesting forth His glory, and justifying His great announcement — 'I am the Light of the world.'

The Four Epiphanies to which the poem refers belong to the Scriptures appointed for the Day itself and the two following Sundays. The first was made to the Wise Men of the East, representing the inspired wisdom of the Gentile world ; the second to the Doctors of the Temple, representing the Bible-taught wisdom of the Jews ; the third to the Forerunner, the last and greatest of the Prophet-heralds of the Incarnation ; the fourth to the Bridegroom and Bride and the wedding guests at Cana of Galilee, representing Humanity, of which the family is the appointed and abiding type.

The Catholic Church by her methods, no less than by her Sacraments, her Scriptures, and her Creeds, is ever maintaining her protest against the limitations by which all merely human systems are disfigured. She is ever bearing her impassioned witness to Him Who is 'the Light that lighteth every man that cometh into the world.' This is the real significance of the solemnities that accompany her Epiphany observance.

NOTE F.

The Gospel Songs.

The Tree of Life is the real Christmas Tree. Its underwoven roots support the cradle; its branches, overarching with many a blossom and many a cluster, form the canopy of the Heavenly Babe, the Darling of God and of man. 'The fruit thereof is for meat, the leaf thereof for medicine;' mindful of which the holy Evangelists speak of the crib as a '*manger*,' that is *the feeding place.* 'Lo! we heard of the same at (Bethlehem) Ephrata, and found it in the Wood.'

The Gospel songs express the joy with which by the humble and simple and pure-hearted this Plant of Renown is discovered;

this House of Bread visited. They come from the lips of a maiden who is a mother, of an ancient who is a child, of a priest who is a prophet. When such fountains of song are unsealed, the music belongs rather to heaven than to earth.

www.ingramcontent.com/pod-product-compliance
Lightning Source LLC
Chambersburg PA
CBHW020040030726
47499CB00007B/2512